COS

COSMOS

LUCIA ODOOM

TRANSLATED BY HUNTER SIMPSON

This paperback edition first published
in the United Kingdom in 2026 by
DAUNT BOOKS
83 Marylebone High Street
London W1U 4QW
publishing@dauntbooks.co.uk

1

This translation has been supported by the Danish Arts Foundation.

First published in Danish by Gads Forlag in 2024

A CIP catalogue record for this title
is available from the British Library

ISBN 978-1-917092-64-7

Typeset by Marsha Swan
Printed and bound in the United Kingdom by Pureprint
www.dauntbookspublishing.co.uk

We, who choose life,
walk one day across the road,
end up in an autumn.
We have the rain, the night, the land
pressed against our hearts
as we walk.

FRANK JÆGER, 'A Promise to Tony'

Sat 13 Aug

Dearest Effie, Aunt Dora, and Pastor Emanuel,

It's about time I wrote to you and put my cards on the table, time I gave you the truth about my life and the Western Union transfers I've been sending. For a while it felt good to send the money, like a way of justifying my daily work, which isn't considered a respectable job here in Copenhagen, where I now find myself. Maybe that's why I haven't replied to your calls and worried messages. I figured that the money spoke for itself.

I'm reading a book about Buddhism and it made me think of you. Pastor Emanuel, please forgive me for embracing another civilisation's spiritual customs, but somehow it feels like the most African thing you can do, seek refuge in other people's heavens.

I close my eyes, willing calmness to wash over me. But I'm in love, I'm hopelessly in love and that's something you can't meditate your way out of. You're probably going to hear more from me about a girl with an elegant neck, a girl I saw just a few weeks ago. Anyway. I don't know if I'm good at meditating, but I'm trying. Apparently the path to Nirvana is suffering, which is something I've been doing for quite a while now, so maybe I'm already halfway there.

I'm going to send you more money today. There's a word in Buddhism, dāna, that means giving a gift without expecting anything in return. It's about generosity. The only thing that makes any sense to me right now is to send you this money – to practise dāna – and try to forget what I had to do to get it.

Let me tell you about the Crows, my Copenhagen family. We make our living collecting the bottles and cans that other people have thrown away. You wouldn't believe how many are thrown away, even though you can turn them in for money at the supermarkets. Odofu, our guiding light, comes from Benin City, and Femi and Kofi are twins from Cape Coast. We meet up almost every day at the city's big library (that's where I am now, writing to you). The library is where most days begin, where we plan our routes and return to for our breaks. We named our WhatsApp group after the crows we see wherever we go. They're very social, and they see gold where others see only rubbish. I read once that crows can even hold a grudge, and that just like us, they know where they're welcome and where they have to stay on their guard. The biggest difference? Crows can cross borders and fly freely. The whole world is their asylum. But we have to settle for the library, a place for books and for outsiders seeking warmth. This is where I found the book on Buddhism, just lying there, glittering with its golden cover.

Odofu is sitting across from me, furtively messaging on his phone. The twins are watching videos on TikTok. Odofu's electric razor is sitting on the next table over, plugged into a socket meant for laptops. He recharges it every day here, even though a guard once told him it was against the rules.

Many homeless people come to this library, people who have a hard time fitting in with Denmark's orderly way of life. They take their shoes off and set up camp, spread newspapers across tables, kick up their feet, hang around all day. No one tells them to leave, but the guard does go around and wake up anyone who's dozed off. Odofu says we should try not to look destitute. Sometimes, after the guard has done his usual round, I sneak in a nap, the hypnotic sound of the escalator lulling me to sleep, reminding me of the waves on the beach back home in Woe.

Sun 14 Aug

Dear Effie, Pastor, and Dora,

While I'm lying in the park, curled up in my sleeping bag, all my belongings tucked in close, I often wonder when the seasons will change. Soon summer will end, and the colder it gets, the harder it will be to earn money. I try to hold on to the warmth, soak it into my soul, store it up for later. And on top of my fear of the coming cold, another unbidden guest stalks my late-night hours: Doubt. It seeps into my skin and cracks my lips no matter how much Vaseline I smear onto them in the day. Why did I leave? My life here is so unpredictable. Should I have stayed with you? I hope that writing to you eases my doubt, my constant companion, the friend that leads me into temptation.

Mon 15 Aug

Dear Effie, Pastor, and Auntie,

There are days when I feel like I've leapt off a very high mountain, thinking I would land in a soft nest of cotton but lately my leap feels more and more like a fall. It's been hard to allow myself to feel the pain of the beating I took when I got to Europe. But the bruises have begun to show, betraying me, evidence of everything I've been through. Admitting how much it hurts to be so far from home is almost too much to bear. But things took a turn a few days ago. I woke up early to collect cans alone. The dawn light wrapped itself around me like an orange blanket as I started working on the outskirts of the city. I rode my bike to the places where the early-bird alcoholics drink beers from 7-Eleven on the benches. By late morning, I had already filled three large bin bags. The night's young partygoers had left bottles on doorsteps and in parks all over the city. There were countless cans with cigarette butts at the bottom, the usual splatters of vomit on the pavements, a flock of pigeons devouring a discarded box of french fries, likely thrown to the ground in a drunken fit. A forgotten shoe was lying beside a rubbish bin. All of Copenhagen is hungover on Saturdays, the ruins of parties littered throughout the usually tidy city, as if there has been a war and everyone's weapon was fast food.

Tue 16 Aug

Hi Effie,

Ever since I got to Copenhagen, I've been paranoid about how I smell and how I look. Am I dirty? Has the journey worn me out, dulled my youthful glow, made me ugly? I'm grey as ashes, and my skin feels rougher than it was back home. My hands are dry as a barren desert landscape with deep grooves running through it. I spent an eternity staring at deodorants on a supermarket shelf, then finally grabbed one that was as tall as a skyscraper. I chose it simply because it was the biggest one (and because it smelled the way I imagine that women want men to smell).

I've been wondering about the worrying lack of smells in Denmark. All the other places I've been to were full of hot, sticky smells, so strong I could taste them. Woe smells like sundried fish, like seaweed and daydreams. But a few days ago, while we were collecting bottles by the beach, the smell of Denmark finally blew in on the wind from the sea: salt and sadness. Later that day, another smell came floating by, the smell that envelops us as we lie down to rest in parks with pockets full of money. A smell I have since identified, while cycling my way through the summer: grass. Newly mown, green grass.

People in this the city are white in a different way than people are white in Italy (where I worked for a few months before I came here). The Danes aren't Mafia-white. It makes me worry that I'm making the city dirty, leaving a trail of filth behind me. Do you remember that movie we watched with uncle Yao, *Trading Places*? Eddie Murphy plays a street hustler who swaps lives with a rich banker in Philadelphia. I've been thinking a lot about the scene where Eddie Murphy steps into a subway car and says: 'Hello, I am Nanga Eboko, exchange student from Cameroon.' We used to joke about that line, Effie, and we would quote it when tourists came to town and talked to us like we were idiots. I'm practising the line in case anyone asks me who I am and what I'm doing in Denmark. I've seriously considered saying: 'Hi, my name is Nanga Eboko and I am an exchange student from Cameroon.'

Wed 17 Aug

Effie, Auntie, and Pastor,

I was thinking about something and I just have to share it with you all. Normally I don't like asking people if I can take their bottles when I'm out collecting, but this morning I summoned up the courage to talk to a couple who were sitting at a table in a park. The sun was showing off, arrogantly optimistic up in the sky. The girl had long brown hair and her legs were slung up on her boyfriend's lap. They were clutching sweaty glass bottles of Coca-Cola, their sunburned faces squinting up at me, smiling kindly. They said it was fine for me to take their bottles, but it turned out that the table they were sitting at belonged to a café that was hidden deeper in the park. As I was walking back to my bike, the two bottles in my hand, the owner of the café came chasing after me. He was shouting, threatening to call the police, repeating, Do you understand what I'm saying to you? It sounded more like a threat than a question. I had been in such a good mood, right up until that moment. Just then, the sky changed its mind and turned grey, and his question rang through my head again and again, What are you even doing here?, weighing me down, along with the simmering sensation of homelessness that I've been repressing for months, even years. But now I'm in love. I know it's temporary. I know it's a distraction, a suspended state that will eventually slide into seriousness. But I want to stay in the house of love just a little longer.

Thu 18 Aug

Dear Effie,

When I saw her for the first time, Copenhagen was still new, unfamiliar. Now I know this city, but in those first few weeks I got lost all the time. I hadn't yet formed a mental map of the capital, and I was walking in confused circles, looking for somewhere to exchange money. One day, I was hit with the unmistakable, comforting smells of coconut, pineapple, shea butter and Dax Wax. Imagine that, in the middle of Denmark's total absence of smells! Hit by the scent of a hair salon, and farther down the street a sign said: Lou's African Style. I stepped out of the grey and into that familiar smell.

I had an instinctive urge to linger in Lou's salon. I realised that no matter where you are in the world, an African hair salon is like an embassy. Long locks hung on the walls – Brazilian, Indian, synthetic. Girls with smooth hair sent me big smiles from shelves full of products that reminded me of you. Olive Oil, Dark and Lovely, concoctions that burn and sting your scalp. I remember you sitting between Aunt Dora's legs, hair full of toxic foam, tears rolling down your cheeks. Then you would put your hair into two braids on each side of your head. That's how I always picture you. Even though it's a hundred hairstyles ago.

She was sitting in the corner of the salon getting her hair braided. I was stealing glances at her reflection in the mirror. She looked so relaxed in that chair in her baggy jumper, engrossed in a book. I could sense her softness and fullness beneath the shirt. African music was playing, Sarkodie. I sang along with 'Adonai' and quickly fell into a conversation with Lou about the song, sneaking looks at her all the while. Her hair was big and knotty below the braids. She was so beautiful as she sat there reading, but I forced myself to stop staring. To focus on Lou. A woman was braiding her hair with a speed that made me dizzy. She was practically shouting into the phone lodged between her breasts as she braided and simultaneously followed along with the soap opera playing on the salon's big flatscreen. A white teenage boy beside her was gritting his teeth as Lou, who usually used his needle to carefully arrange long locks of hair, gave him dreads.

Lou is from the Ivory Coast, and has thin dreads himself. He told me he gets all his music from another hair stylist in the neighborhood who always comes back from Ghana with bolts of fabric, homemade hair bonnets, and USB sticks full of new songs. He tried to sell me one of the bonnets, saying it was made of silk, but I politely declined. Instead, I asked him if he knew where I could go to exchange and send money. He said I should try down at the train station, and he told me which buses went there. There was a bus stop right outside the salon, I could just hop on. Lou gave me 25 kroner for a ticket, even though I hadn't asked him for it, and he said I should come back soon to get my hair cut. First time's on the house, he said with a wink. I took it as a polite suggestion.

Before I left the salon, she took out her earphones and asked Lou who had sprayed deodorant everywhere. Her words haunted me all the way to the station.

Fri 19 Aug

Dear Pastor, Effie, and Dora,

I've got €25 burning a hole in my pocket, like a bonfire that will turn all my worries into a heap of ashes. It's a miracle that we can earn money just from picking up cans and bottles and putting them into a big machine that looks like a gaping mouth with a rolling tongue. You have to lay them carefully into its big jaws, and you've got to do it just right, or the machine will spit them back out again. You can't rush it. Its tongue pulls the cans and bottles down its throat, and when you're done feeding the mouth, a little piece of paper comes out with an amount written on it that you can redeem for cash at the supermarket's registers. Every time I walk up with my receipt I meet the same lady, who looks at me from behind her register, unimpressed. She ought to see a lottery winner standing in front of her, but instead she looks at me with pity.

I sent you a little money from today's bottle harvest, but I'm scraping more together for something important. I'm lying in a park right now,

Femi and Kofi are dancing to the sound of their speaker, and Odofu is rubbing himself with body lotion. Like you, Pastor, he massages it into his skin with the care of a rich man in Accra washing his car. He finishes his moisturising ritual by spraying himself with the Paco Rabanne perfume that he's obsessed with.

We're in the park where we sleep every night, Folkets Park, where we know we're guests, a place that belongs to drug dealers, teenagers, and families with young children. They all have their separate corners of the park, and we lie under the trees, knowing that everyone wishes we would pack our things and go.

Sun 21 Aug

Dear Pastor, Effie, and Dora,

Today is going to be a good day. I just woke up with dew on my eyelids. Sunlight filled my eyes when I opened them, and I thought of you. You'll be awake by now, your day already begun. You're probably sitting around the table, eating cornflakes and fresh fruit, dipping bread into your tea. Pastor, you're trying to hide the fact that you've poured Ovaltine cocoa powder in your cup instead of tea, but there's no getting anything by you, Auntie, though you often let us get away with our mischief. You're picking the seeds from a watermelon and passing the pieces over to Effie. The fishermen have probably pushed out to sea, and the women are waiting for them to come back in with today's catch. When they've chosen their fish, they'll spend the whole day drying them in the sun. The fish will lie on the ground like tourists in beach chairs, tanning themselves until their skin turns red. I grasp for you with the fishing net of my thoughts. If I were with you, I would sit in your shop, Auntie, drink Ovaltine, and sneak over to swipe a few snacks. Then I'd stroll over to Uncle Yao's salon to watch a football match. But the sun is the only thing I have with me from home, and in a few months it will disappear, with only the wind and the cold to step into its place.

I'm scraping money together to buy a house for you, Effie. Your house will have a big living room with a stone floor, a sofa, a recliner for Pastor, and a television for Aunt Dora, and there will be enough room for your child to play and jump around. I can picture the porch, which I'll build myself, and your kitchen and your bedroom, Effie, and a room for me to live in when I come back home. In your garden there will be cabbage, okra, carrots, peppers, spring onions, maybe chili peppers. There will be enough vegetables for you to be self-sufficient. You'll have a henhouse with hens to bless you with fresh eggs and meat.

The Crows talk a lot about what to do when the sun goes into hibernation. Maybe my visa from Italy will help me get better paying work in Copenhagen, but everything's so uncertain.

Tue 23 Aug

Hi Effie,

I owe you an explanation for what I wrote about being in love. I bet you've been rolling your eyes at the fact that I haven't supplied any juicier details. Do you remember what I wrote about the woman who was reading in Lou's salon? Ever since then, I've been hoping to see her again. I dreamed up a thousand ways I could make up for my excessive deodorant use.

Well, something unexpected happened on Friday afternoon when we marched over to Rådhuspladsen hoping to find lots of bottles. Luck hasn't been on our side lately, we've been earning too little. We keep procrastinating, each video we watch online lures us on to another, pulling time out from under us. We fly on the magic carpet of distraction, dozing in the grass, and now we only have a few months to earn as much money as possible. The twins and I are here on work permits, a nulla osta al lavoro, a plaster on the wounds left by a hellish period of endless, unpaid labour on the tomato farms of Puglia. We have to scrape money together fast, before time runs out. So we had both high hopes and frayed nerves that day, because we heard that there was going to be an African demonstration at Rådhuspladsen, and that there would probably be lots of bottles to collect.

We walked through a flock of pigeons, which flew up like confetti as we made our way over to the crowd of people. That's when I saw her, the woman from the salon. This time she had her hair up, revealing her long neck, a neck like those that elegantly rise in all the cities of Ghana, women with buckets on their heads and children on their backs. She was taking pictures of the people around her with a camera while a guy in a brown corduroy jacket captivated everyone from the stage.

It's always best to keep quiet instead of telling a woman what you're thinking. I ought to have learned that by now. Odofu has taught me the unspoken rules of Danish society while I've been here, how you shouldn't try to talk to people you don't know, how it takes time to figure out whether you're friends with someone or just acquaintances, and how the natives are always the ones who set these parameters. He also taught me to never try to seek eye contact, and to never act cocky. But I couldn't help flirting with her. It was bad, Effie. I grew painfully aware of how dirty my hands always were, so I stuffed them into my pockets as I nodded to her, and she nodded back. I asked her name, and what the demonstration was about. She stuck her hand out, so I had no choice but to offer her mine, which had been inside every single one of the city's bins. She said her name was Elizabeth, her eyes were warm, her hands soft as silk. I held on for too long, and called her 'Queen Elizabeth' taking a bow. She gave a hoarse laugh and told me I was corny. You'd be the first to agree with her about that, Effie.

I asked where she was from. I was sure she was East African, and I nodded triumphantly when she told me she was Tanzanian. She looked at me inquisitively and asked if I was from Nigeria. You've got that Nigerian confidence, she said, which I took as a compliment, and she laughed when I told her I was Ghanaian with Nigerian attitude. Elizabeth looked at my bags, but fortunately she looked at me, too, in that way that women often do. I don't mean to brag, Effie, but you yourself have always said that you didn't like having me around your friends, that I steal their attention. I was relieved that she checked me out. At least I'm pretty sure she did.

She said it was a demonstration in solidarity with refugees, and she started telling me about a shipwreck off the coast of Greece, and how it had happened so many times now that it didn't make much of an impression on Europeans anymore. While she was talking, I thought of the waves and the baking sun up in the sky and the angry sea that had pulled at us from both sides. Her words ricocheted through my body, and I couldn't resist interrupting her to tell her I had also been out there on the Mediterranean, in danger, on the way to Europe.

She asked me where I had sailed from and who had organised the journey. She was cautious at first, but then she prodded me a bit, saying she didn't understand how I could put my life and fate in unknown hands. She had stopped waiting for me to reply, she just talked faster and faster about how careless it was to pay strangers to put my life in danger. I smiled, which just wound her up more, and she said there was nothing to find in Europe, 'the mirage of the West', and when I asked what she was doing here herself, she just glared back at me. I felt like I'd won a battle. Silence hung between us for a while, and then she apologised. But I didn't mind, I'd been admiring her the whole time she was lecturing me.

I asked her about the speaker, who everyone was paying attention to except us. She told me it was Eugene, who had been a close friend of hers for many years. Her voice grew warmer as she spoke about him, how he brings people together with his words and energy. I praised his speech while wondering whether Eugene was more than just her friend. She grabbed my arm, gave it a squeeze, said she was glad I came. Since that day I've been hoping she would lecture me again.

When we left Rådhuspladsen, Odofu kept looking at me suspiciously. There hadn't been many bottles to go after, so he couldn't see why I had that goofy smile. But then he gave me a nudge and said that he thought there were more beautiful women at that demonstration than he'd seen in all his time in Europe, trying to provoke a reaction. I didn't take the bait, but for the rest of the day Elizabeth's face swam before me, her moods shifting within it.

Fri 26 Aug

Dear Effie, Pastor Emanuel, and Dora

Odofu has taught me how to be tactful when asking people for their cans and bottles, how to use my natural charm instead of barging into conversations. The Danes sit on picnic blankets under shady trees or out on the grass, they drink beer, play games, listen to music on their speakers, make the most of summer. I glide between groups, following Odofu's tried and tested instructions: don't smile too much and never look them in the eye, but it's a good idea to toss out a little joke, something along the lines of: 'I'm just trying to save the planet', which is Odofu's go-to. It's also best if you distance yourself from any kind of suffering. People ignore the shabbiest-looking collectors. You get punished for killing the vibe. That's why I try to stay clean and dress well. I smile, but not too much. It's always a good strategy to appeal to their guilty consciences about the environment. To look like someone fighting for their life is the worst thing you can do.

New crows arrive in Copenhagen all the time. They, too, come here from southern Europe with broken wings. We nod to one another on the bike lanes, in the parks, and on the street. Are they hiding behind WhatsApp, too? Do their families know what they're doing here? How they really are? How they beg, make their living from rubbish, and sleep without a roof over their heads?

Sat 27 Aug

Hi Effie,

This morning Elizabeth came walking across Queen Louise's Bridge while the twins were dancing to a Tyla song that a young guy was playing on a loudspeaker. I've already seen her a few times since the demonstration, but she hasn't noticed me. She's always been too far away for me to wave or call her name. Today she looked back over her shoulder and it seemed like she saw me, but she just kept walking. Her braids hung down to her hips, she had her camera around her neck, deep in conversation with a girlfriend. They walked arm in arm in that slow way that only Africans can walk. I swallowed my pride and ran after her, and she seemed happy when I tapped her shoulder. Maybe she just didn't recognise me earlier? Or maybe she isn't interested in me at all? I tried to suppress these thoughts as I gave her my number while her friend looked on, fascinated. Femi clapped his hands as I walked back triumphantly, holding my phone in the air like a trophy.

Imagine my shock when a message from Elizabeth popped up on my phone a moment ago. It was a gif of Kobe Bryant flying through the air, and she asked me if I could see how much I look like him. I wrote back that I don't look a bit like Kobe (may he rest in peace), but that I was flattered. Half an hour went by until her next message. She wrote that she knows a basketball court that's almost always open. I responded that I would love to meet her there for a game, but I wouldn't show any mercy just because she was a lady with short legs. She replied with a gif of Allen Iverson jumping up to give Michael Jordan a chest bump.

Sun 28 Aug

Dearest Effie,

You must've given birth by now, because you were three months pregnant when I got home from the cashew plantations in Bono. It was obvious at the time that there was something you didn't dare to tell me. You had started wearing flowy dresses, and you complained about feeling seasick all the time. Even in Bono I could tell that something was up. I shouldn't have gone to the cashew plantations. I shouldn't have asked Myles to keep an eye on you. I should never have trusted him. But before I left, I got the sense he'd grown out of his immature ways with women. He'd got himself a full-time job working for a coffin maker, and he talked about the Bible all the time. But this was right after he had an affair with a missionary, so I probably should've realised that all his Jesus talk was just a pick-up line and not an actual revelation. He stopped answering my calls and messages, and I know what that means, I understand men. The gods know that I don't have a clean conscience, but now at least I can build a house for you and your baby. This is my way of trying to fix things. Here's a meme of Will Smith slapping Chris Rock. If I ever see Myles again, I'll do the same to him.

Mon 29 Aug

Dear Effie, Pastor, and Auntie,

We're sitting on Queen Louise's Bridge because Femi wanted to watch girls go by, but we've mostly just been staring at our phones. The twins are transfixed by a Nigerian woman with 200,000 followers on Instagram. She shares her humble life with people all over the world, and she's received so much money in donations that her whole standard of living has improved. The first evidence of this was a purple, velour bedframe, then came all the boxes that she unpacks daily for her followers: beauty products, clothes, wigs. Kofi says she's going to move into a room with a private bathroom and a TV soon; she used to live in a spartan cabin! An anonymous female follower has paid for it all. In her most popular videos, she shows how she cooks her meals outside on an open flame. She always washes the meat, which for some reason is astonishing to Westerners. Her followers love to see her washing clothes in a bucket or sitting on the floor eating. They're fascinated by her minimal resources and positive outlook. The twins say that she's successful because she's willing to put her poverty on display, she knows it's her ticket out, and now her followers want to see her new and improved life. But Odofu says she should be careful not to seem too lucky, because then she'd lose the appeal that got her here in the first place. He loves to go on about how important dignity is. He thinks it gets people to show more empathy, whereas the beggars who look dirty and shabby repel people. But at the end of the day we're all beggars.

We watch a video of the Nigerian woman drinking her daily bag of ice water while telling her followers in a voiceover how much she's looking forward to moving. She thanks God for her blessings. We also see her buy rice at a market as she explains how the prices have skyrocketed.

We all know that we have more in common with her than we would ever dare admit to ourselves, or to each other. The big difference between her and us is that the world comes to her. In the comments section, several of her followers offer to donate money after they learn that a kilo of rice costs €15 in Nigeria. Kofi says that her followers are buying shares in her life, investing in her, wielding power over her fate. Femi says she's just selling her poverty to get rich, but Kofi disagrees, he thinks it's both clever and brave that she can earn money just by existing. They continue arguing as we keep watching one video after another, gazing on with homesickness and longing as she cooks a banku and okra stew.

The twins are both incredibly stubborn, but Femi is the one who usually gets his way, mainly because he's the more dramatic of the two, wearing his opponent down; that reminds me of a certain someone I know, Effie. The other day they got into a fight over a girl who they had each felt chemistry with at a party. They both got her number, and they decided to let the best man win. They spent the whole day trying to out-flirt each other over Messenger. I tried to tell them it wasn't going to end well for either one of them, but they refused to listen, and they persisted until the poor girl blocked them both.

Tue 30 Aug

Dear Pastor, Effie, and Aunt Dora,

Have I ever told you about my job in Bono? Before I left, it felt like time had been standing still for much too long, like I was getting older and younger at the same time, just waiting to be carried out by the tide. I felt depressed and aimless. But Yao told me that there was seasonal work in the Bono region, where they grow corn, yams, plantains, cocoa fruit, mangoes, and cashews. I was hired because the region had started a project to help the cashew plantations reduce waste among their crops. The area around the trees had to be carefully tended. Now that I think about it, maybe that was my first meditative experience. There was a team of us who had to rake the soil beneath the trees so that the fruits hiding the cashew nuts could have the best conditions to grow in. It had been a long time since something felt so meaningful, like entering into a significant cycle. The fruit has to dry in the sun before you can open it and peel out the nuts, ever so gently. They were always telling us that we weren't actually dealing with nuts, but seeds. Cashew seeds look like a little kidney, and our boss joked that they were almost as valuable as a human kidney, as we very carefully removed the seeds from the fruits and rinsed away the sticky oil surrounding them like glue. The nut must be completely clean or its price will plummet, and this is often where things go wrong, during the rinsing, because far too many nuts are lost to impatient hands. The early phase of the process is crucial. It may be laborious, but the pay is good, to ensure that the workers will do their best.

I always dreamed of becoming a fisherman like Dad, but there wasn't enough work, and for the first time in ages I actually felt useful. I met lots of men in Bono who had been to Europe, Qatar, America, or Asia. They showed me pictures of the houses they had built for their families, and told me how the money they earned had helped pay for school and books for siblings, nephews, and nieces. I listened to their stories while discarding all of their warnings, as if they were the fruit around a cashew seed. I focused on everything these men now possessed. When I got home from Bono, I wanted to make sure that you would be all right, Effie. So before I left for Italy, I bought some land with the money I had saved up in Bono. The next step is to lay the foundation. I've already drawn up the plans, and I'll send them to you after this message.

Wed 31 Aug

Dear Auntie, Uncle, and Effie,

Elizabeth destroyed me. We met in the orange summer light on a big basketball court behind a school. She brought her ball in a Spalding bag, and was wearing a big jumper and a pair of shorts she was practically drowning in. Elizabeth plays like a sniper and moves like a dancer. I lost myself in her movements. Her braids hit me with a smack as she dribbled with sharp, sneaky motions. She glided past me as if it were the easiest thing in the world. She stole the ball from me without seeming to make the slightest effort. Needless to say, I lost. She confessed that she had played on the national youth team, but her dreams were crushed by a serious knee injury. Afterwards, we sat on the court drinking Cokes and eating Pringles while I stewed like a sore loser. I took my shirt off, a cheap trick, but I was a defeated man, and it seemed to work. There he is again, that corny guy, she smiled, but I could tell she was looking at me even though she tried to hide it. She rifled through her bag and told me she had taken a photo of me at the demonstration before we met. I thought I was the one who saw her first that day at Rådhuspladsen, but she pulled out a photograph of me looking up at the stage with my bags sitting in front of me, my head slightly tilted and my arms crossed. This was the first time we met, she said. Not exactly, I said, and I told her how I saw her at the hair salon. So you're the one who reeked of Axe! she shouted.

Mon 5 Sep

Dearest Effie, Auntie, and Pastor,

Today Femi was accosted by an older bottle collector with a ratty grey backpack. He yelled at him in Danish, but you didn't need to understand the language to know that it wasn't a friendly greeting coming out of his mouth. Femi was just about to start shouting back at the man, but then Kofi walked over and helped him fish some bottles out of the bin Femi had been sifting through. Kofi patted the man on the back and said ha' en god dag og pas på dig selv, have a good day and take care of yourself. This got Femi more riled up – Kofi's ability to defuse situations only makes Femi want to blow everything up even more.

Femi is the brazen twin, Kofi the contemplative and quiet one. He's the one who works things out when Femi gets into arguments with the wrong people. When the gangs tell us to get lost from the park where we sleep, or when they yell at us for collecting bottles and cans on their turf, Femi gets furious, but Kofi usually manages to settle everybody down again.

The first time I saw them was when I was working on the tomato farm in Italy. A crowd was gathered in the camp that we paid almost our whole salary to live in. At its centre, Femi and Kofi were dancing, beautifully in sync with each other, right in the middle of that slum where we were supposed to get our rest but instead slept with one eye open every night. While I was admiring their moves, they asked me if I would help film them. Their plan was to become TikTok famous.

Their dances were always a highlight after the long exhausting hours out in the fields, under the merciless sun. The twins already knew Odofu. With cuts on his arms and legs and a black eye, his punishment for daring to complain about our low pay and poor working conditions, he was hard to miss. He's the one who heard about Copenhagen from a friend who returned home from here last year. We planned our route and put our meagre earnings together to bribe a higher-up so we could move on and find better pay elsewhere. I don't know what I would've done without them. With each other's hands we hold the days together.

Thu 8 Sep

Dear Effie,

I ran into Elizabeth again today. She was wearing a kerchief and a long thin coat. It was pouring with rain and I was draped in a big green rain poncho, but she recognised me all the same, standing there at an intersection with my bike, looking for shelter. She ran towards me with her big umbrella open above her head and wrapped an arm around me, stood up on her tiptoes, kissed me on the cheek. I could feel my muscles beneath my clothes, all the soreness, all my nerves and bruises, everything vanished with her touch. We went into a Turkish restaurant with a rotating kebab and freshly baked pita bread. We talked for hours as the rain thrummed against the windowpane. She teased me for being the type of person who eats what's on their plate methodically; first I ate the round mountain of rice, then the salad and the peppers on my kebab skewer, and finally the meat. Between bites, she took hold of my hands and rubbed them with hers. She tilted her head and asked me about my family. I told her about you, Effie, about your quick wit and how close we are. I even told her about Mum and Dad's car accident, how they died a few years after we had moved to Woe, how we only moved there because Dad couldn't make a living as a fisherman in Accra.

My descriptions of the huge mountains of abandoned clothes that lie like rubbish on the beach in Accra made a strong impression on Elizabeth. It all comes from Europe, from the chains that mass-produce clothes and then dump tonnes of their unsold products in the country's poorest places. I told her how the clothes drift out into the ocean and choke the fish. She shook her head when I explained how our father had to sail for two days to get to the places where there were still fish in the sea. And when I told her how we played on the great big mountains of clothes when we were kids, as we waited for our father to come home, she just looked down. I also told her how happy we were when we moved to Woe, closer to Pastor Emanuel and Aunt Dora, even though we had very little space. Fish was in high demand, and it was hard work for Dad, but we were grateful. I also mentioned the day when you, my beautiful sister, dragged me down to the beach to tell off a young fisherman who treated you badly, disappearing just days after bombarding you with declarations of love. Do you remember how you yelled at him in front of all the other fishermen, even his captain, who couldn't help but laugh at the whole drama? The tide carried the fishermen far away from all the women, the mothers, daughters, sisters, and you were cursing him on behalf of every woman who'd ever had to wait on that beach, staring out to sea.

Elizabeth said she was sure that she and you would get along well. She told me that she's not the silently suffering type either, that she loses it if a man keeps her waiting. I hope I'll get to find out what she wants. I let my impatience and curiosity run away with me, and I asked if she had only ever had Danish or white boyfriends. She nodded with that mysterious expression of hers and told me about her last boyfriend. They were together for two years, and he was always saying that he didn't see the colour of her skin. She said it was like he erased her with that sentence. Why did he feel the need to look away from the very thing she couldn't conceal from the world?

After we left the restaurant, we had a long hug goodbye. I really did try not to lean down and kiss her, but after a while I couldn't resist the temptation, and I did it. She pushed me away gently with the palms of her hands, but then, right when I was about to back away, she pulled me in closer.

Fri 9 Sep

Dearest Effie, Aunt Dora, and Pastor Emanuel,

It's Monday and the morning's tears flow down silent windowpanes. The city wakes up, slowly fills with bikes drifting down special lanes reserved for them alone. The cyclists move like big schools of fish with their children perched behind them and headphones in their ears and expressionless faces. The drinkers, whether it's beer, Coke, or Lucozade, don't start dumping bottles until lunchtime. I'm always sure to check the rubbish bins near schools, and it's important to keep an eye out for groups of teenagers coming back from the shops with their energy drinks and snacks, because they're usually willing to give me their empty cans. Then I hurry on to the next school from one end of the city to the other, looking through containers and more bins and sorting the bottles from the cans.

Thursday through Sunday is when Copenhagen comes to life. On these days you can find more bottles, remnants of gatherings between friends and lovers, sometimes a whole case of empties. The cases are the hardest things to get your hands on, because often people themselves go and exchange them for money to buy more beer. But sometimes we're lucky. Odofu has taught us everything he knows about the city's rhythms and how to follow them to earn the most money. After we meet in the morning, we all cycle off in different directions.

I cover the whole city every day, and I come very close to people I'll never know. I observe them walking down the street with their brand-new jeans and their laptop bags. I watch them talking on their phones, going for a run, shopping with their children, and sitting in their cars on the way out of town, maybe heading to the airport for a holiday. Some wear cropped jackets and others wear long coats, they interpret the weather differently, stop and wait for the traffic light to turn green. They swing bags of new clothes, they own apartments, furniture, they have money in their bank accounts and calendars with plans written on them. And they've already decided who I am. They barely even look my way, so I'm free to keep staring, to really study them, their nonchalance, the effortless way they move through their days. All sorts of things happen in their lives that will never happen in mine. It's exactly the same feeling I have when I watch a movie and fantasise about breaking through the screen and stepping into the story.

Sun 11 Sep

Dear Effie,

Today Elizabeth wanted to teach me to swim in the ice-cold sea. I thought she'd lost her mind. We had just finished a game of basketball, and she said a dip would do us good. I summoned up the courage to tell her that I can't swim, and that I thought it was way too cold anyway. But she just shrugged and said there was nothing she would rather do than teach me how to swim. The sea gives the biggest embrace you can get, she said, putting her arm around me, our sweat a glue binding us together. I wanted to tell her about all the breaths the sea has stolen, but I kept it to myself.

When we got to the beach, I cautiously dipped my foot into the water. It may as well have been acid. I focused on all the stranded jellyfish lying transparent and sticky in the sand, clinging to dry land, as if they knew the sea was no place for amateurs. The moment I felt the water graze my foot, a chill ran through me. I've tried to hide my queasy days at sea away in the back of my mind, but standing at the water's edge, my bones, my skin, and my nerves suddenly remembered the boat. How at first glance it looked far too small to fit all the people waiting to get on board with their few possessions. Most of us were young men in our twenties and thirties, but there was also a lone woman travelling with her teenage son. She didn't look much older than him, and she had probably had him when she herself was a teenager. The sight of them made me think of you, Effie. There was a silence among us as we walked on board, a shared knowledge that this journey came with no guarantee of a final destination. The boat could become our coffin. People have been pulled down to the sea floor, ships and planes, mountains, entire civilisations, soldiers and Africans are lying down there. Sea creatures move into these sunken hulls, these cemeteries. Our forefathers and foremothers were taken from their families, and some of them never saw land again before they vanished into the water. The sea is a gateway to heaven and a chasm to hell.

As soon as we pushed off, the whole world turned to sea. Time blurred its boundaries between the hours and the days. I remember extreme seasickness and the sky swaying above me. I passed the time by thinking, sometimes way too much, but other times my head was empty. I wondered whether the sea had a bottom or if I would drift down forever into the deep, black nothingness and drown.

I remember the taste of canned baked beans, vomit, and my dry, salty mouth. Water in bottles that always tasted slightly salty. Constant dizziness and the sloshing of the waves. Having damp clothes on and trying to relax instead of panicking. How we emptied our stomachs in the boat, which stank of desperate hollow bellies. I don't remember any of my fellow passengers' faces, and I don't remember how long we were at sea either. It could've been days, weeks, or a whole month. But I knew that my birthday fell somewhere within that stream of time. The words Cosmos was 33 years old came into my mind, he was only 33 years old.

After leaving Woe and taking bus after bus, hitchhiking and walking, popping a thousand blisters, regretting and doubting, there I was, at sea, in that little boat that seemed so fragile. I floated out there between existence and obliteration, and I became aware of my own insignificant place in the world. But I also reminded myself of the thrill of motion. Of moving my body with my own strength. In my thoughts I tried to move one foot in front of the other, but I felt so alone. When we finally saw the lifeboat approaching, I looked into Odofu's eyes, and his relief flowed into me. After that, I promised myself that I would stick with him wherever he went.

Elizabeth's eyes were one with the sun as she pulled me out into the cold sea. Water dripped reluctantly from her skin, the drops refusing to let go of her. The sun's rays unfurled a red carpet for us from the shore out into the water. She had her braids tied up in a bun like a pineapple on top of her head. First she tried to teach me how to float, but it was in vain. She told me to relax my whole body and feel my legs floating upward. But all that happened was that I sank in the water like a stone. In the end, Elizabeth held me up, and the sky and the sea held me too. I loved her in that moment, Effie, suspended in the sea, the very same sea that had threatened to swallow me when I travelled from Libya. I pulled her close, and she pulled me underwater. I kissed her legs and her belly, and we played like sea creatures until a family came walking out onto the dock with a dog on a leash.

Effie, do you remember how Pastor Emanuel used to take me with him on his missions to Akosombo? As I was floating there in the water, I thought of the boys who fished with their bodies. They were as young as seven years old when they were sold by their parents and put to work for the fishermen on Lake Volta. They dove into the dark water from little wooden boats, and they were like a part of the lake themselves, almost godlike. I held my breath when I saw them jump in and dive underwater, but by the time their heads appeared on the surface I had long since started breathing again. Pastor Emanuel often went to Akosombo to try to get these boys returned to their parents, who regretted selling their children. But not all of the boys wanted to go home again. It was as if they already felt more at home there in the water with each other.

Mon 12 Sep

Dear Effie, Auntie, and Pastor,

I'm not ready to tell Elizabeth about my journey to Europe, about the suffering she might sympathise with but can't possibly understand. I don't want her to pity me. But it's a relief to share it all with you.

On the day I left home, I didn't even say goodbye. I woke up and looked around my room as the dawn light slowly broke through the window. I drank it all in, fearing I wouldn't be able to remember it again: the pink mosquito net, my chest of drawers, my bed. I packed a little duffel bag with only the bare necessities: two phones (one smartphone and one old Nokia), five phone cards, some clothes, two books – the Bible and The Palm-Wine Drinkard, your favourite book, pastor (the copy you gave me, but which I never read) – a few chargers, a little wooden figurine from Aunt Dora, and a big, sweet loaf of bread.

Only the sea was awake. It lay out there whispering to me and I followed its voice as I moved through the house. Everything else was silent, even the hens hadn't yet begun their clucking. The smell of boiled goat meat and banku from the night before hung in the living room, and I inhaled deeply. Then I walked out the door with light steps, down to the garden gate, which always creaked and squeaked. Instead of opening it, I jumped over soundlessly. I continued eagerly down the gravel path, impatient, unable to grasp how long the road ahead would be. I walked past the houses of the town, and along its ditches swimming with little tadpoles, breathless, barely able to contain my excitement as I left one house after another behind me. Everything around me was wrapped in a wonderful pink light: the little grocery store with its Coca-Cola sign; Yao's home, with its goats and its henhouse and its illustrations of hairstyles that hadn't been updated since the 1990s. There was sorrow in the silence, so I took out my headphones and let 'Could You Be Loved' hold my hand. As I put Woe behind me, I didn't dare look back at the lighthouse looming above the palms at the edge of the beach. Soon the rooster would start crowing and the boats would be pushed out over the waves. I left our town before little stalls and businesses in the market opened, before the streets started swarming with schoolchildren in brown and yellow uniforms.

I imagined your footsteps on the gravel, Effie. Our forefathers gave me wind at my back, their hands rested on my shoulders. I didn't dare to wake you before I left, to feel your skin against mine, it would have only bound me forever to the red soil of Woe. I don't think I've ever been happier and stupider than I was on that morning, walking down the road with music in my ears as the sun rose up, hopeful and alone.

Sat 17 Sep

Dear Effie,

Odofu confronted me yesterday evening. He said I seemed distant lately. He said I'd been neglecting the Crows, pushing them away and allowing myself to be lulled into the fantasy of a relationship with Elizabeth. He called me, because I hadn't been answering my texts. When I answered the phone, he was practically yelling, What does the word friendship mean to you, Cosmos? And I understood exactly what he meant. We were lucky, because although we had been in such humiliating situations, we had been in them together. When the police stop us on the street and demand to see our papers, we are each other's witnesses, and when passers-by on the street dismiss us, ridicule us, yell at us, or threaten us, we are each other's witnesses, and when we have no idea what to do, one of us will always pick up the phone. Odofu has guided me through the world by the hand, and now I've let go of that hand and taken hold of another. It isn't a betrayal that I fell in love; it's a betrayal that I let my love get in the way of our friendship. When I'm with Elizabeth, I don't just forget Odofu, but myself, too. Time collapses and I forget all about the past and the future.

Sun 18 Sep

Dear Effie,

Elizabeth rests her head on my shoulder when we sit together on the basketball court, her bare skin against mine. She puts her arm around me when we walk down the street, and she no longer lets go of me when we run into people she knows. She touches me, no longer scared, no longer hesitant and restrained. She dribbles the ball in my direction over and over; she's even started letting me win. I can tell that's what she wants, for me to win, and she lets me steal the ball so she can reward me with a kiss. But these days with Elizabeth are beginning to eat into each other, almost becoming one. Soon I have to pay for the materials for your house, which means I've got to find work that pays better than bottle collecting. I only have one month to get the first thousand euros together, otherwise construction will grind to a halt. We've both seen those building projects that stall and deteriorate, and we know how expensive it is when that happens. I showed Elizabeth my plans for your little house, and she kissed my cheek and said it looked beautiful. She liked the peach I picked out for you, almost your favourite colour, pink.

Thu 22 Sep

Dear Pastor Emanuel, Auntie, and Effie

There are schisms in our clan of Crows. Today we were sitting on some steps, enjoying the last rays of sun, and I could feel Odofu's eyes on me. I pretended not to notice, but then he said something I can't stop thinking about. 'You're very handsome, Cosmos,' and it sounded like a declaration of love, but a coldness crept into his words as he went on. 'Your beauty is your passport, it opens doors for you, it shades you from the sun. You can fly on the wings of your face.' The twins, who had been glued to a football match on their phone, looked up, suddenly losing interest in the game. Odofu delivered a lengthy speech about how my looks had granted me acceptance and refuge, and how he had noticed that people gladly handed their bottles over to me with courteous smiles, as if they were happy to be graced by my presence. I don't know why he's so mad, he is hardly an ugly man, with his strong jaw and rugged yet rough face, rougher than mine and the twins', making him look older, weathered yet striking.

Odofu's words stung. I know exactly what he was trying to say. I also feel the distance that's come between us since I met Elizabeth, catapulting me into a totally different world than the Crows.

Sat 24 Sep

Dear Effie,

I haven't spoken to Odofu for a few days. I'm lying in Elizabeth's bed, and I can't sleep. I keep thinking about something that I don't think our uncle has ever told you himself. Try to imagine Pastor Emanuel's deep, calm voice as you read this story about his time in London and how he got his legendary name, becoming Pastor Emanuel even though he wasn't an actual priest and he didn't believe in the God of the white people.

Pastor was heartbroken over a Christian girl named Debbie, who was only with him to upset her old, conservative, Thatcher-supporting parents before dropping him in favour of a more respectable British officer. Pastor's dream of a life in London was slipping through his fingers, and none of his plans for the future seemed to be within reach. He had to move out of Debbie's apartment, and he drowned his sorrows with some hard drinking. He went out with two friends he'd met during the Brixton uprising, stumbling from pub to pub, and he ended up back at one of their apartments, where they listened to The Ethiopians as loud as their speakers could go and drank and drank until they fell asleep, marinated in a mixture of rum, palm wine, green bananas, and tobacco. The room kept growing smokier long after the last joint had gone around and Pastor Emanuel had passed out cold.

In his drunken sleep that night, Pastor Emanuel dreamed he was travelling with his grandfather to Zambia to fish in Lake Bangweulu. His grandfather caught a big, silver fish with a discontented expression on its face. The corners of its mouth hung down just like Queen Elizabeth's did, which always made her look so sullen. His grandfather held eye contact with the fish for what felt like minutes, and then frantically cast it back into the water. Afterwards, they hurried away from the lake, and as they drove home the darkness grew dense. All along, Pastor Emanuel had a vision of the fish with the sad, dead eyes. At a certain point, it got so dark that they couldn't see a thing. They drifted across the motorway until the car ran right into a sycamore tree and burst into flames, lighting up the flat landscape around them. Pastor Emanuel struggled for a long time to get out of the car, and just when it seemed hopeless and his strength was about to fail him, the sky lit up for a split second with a beautiful orange burst of light, and then all the trees on the plain caught fire. A figure emerged from the flames. An angel of death in the guise of a fish, its scales a thousand shades of shimmering silver. The fish god stared at them for a long time, its sad, penetrating gaze moving from one to the other, before it decisively fixed its eyes on Pastor Emanuel's grandfather. Then it transformed into the lighthouse in Woe.

Pastor Emanuel woke up with thick smoke in his nostrils. The apartment was in flames and he had to call the fire department, but miraculously they all made it out unscathed. He must've fallen asleep with a lit cigarette in his hand. It turned out that his grandfather in Woe died that very night, and it was said that the dark sky over the sea lit up with a flash of orange light as he breathed his last breath.

After that night, our uncle left the liquor on the shelf, and a few months later, he went home to Woe, where he founded the Church of African Folk Spirituality and started writing books on African religions. And that's why everyone calls him Pastor Emanuel.

Tue 27 Sep

Dear Effie,

Today my search for bottles brought me to the beach. It reminds me a little of our favourite beach in Woe where the lighthouse stands, guiding boats around the mountain in the water, the fabled mountain that no one's seen but everybody fears. It's nearly deserted here, so I'm spending my day with the sea, which greets me like an old friend. Before you were born, Dad would send me down to keep an eye on the sea, asking me to tell him what mood it was in every morning before he sailed out. I would stand on the shore and wave to him until he was just a little speck in the distance: 'The sea is in a good mood today, Daddy', 'the sea is resting, Daddy', 'the sea has a tummyache, Daddy'. If the sea had a tummyache it meant that the wind was high, so Dad would wait to sail out and we would spend the day together instead. We passed the time looking for little turtles and starfish as we walked in silence down the windy beach.

Thu 29 Sep

Hi again Effie,

Elizabeth invited me along to a poetry reading tonight. She's noticed me writing on my phone when we take breaks from playing basketball. I put up a lot of resistance, but in the end I relented and agreed to recite one of my poems at the reading. It's called 'The Flaming Fish' and, as you can probably guess, it's about Pastor Emanuel's revelation. I'd been thinking about reading it aloud for the Crows, but ever since Odofu lectured me about my good fortune, my beauty, and all the possibilities it brings me, I've been too embarrassed to do it.

When I got to the reading, Elizabeth's friend Eugene was at the bar. Beside him was a guy, or at least I think he was a guy – he was both feminine and masculine – and I'm pretty sure he checked me out. Kvæde, he said, holding out his hand to me. I asked him self-consciously to repeat that, because I have a hard time pronouncing the vowel Æ, a sound you often hear when the Danes are talking. It reminds me of the 'eh' sound the aunties make when they order us around. Kvæde laughed at my many attempts to pronounce his name. Eugene could tell how nervous I was and he pulled me outside to smoke. I'm not sure why I took a cigarette from him, because I don't smoke. I was supposed to read last, and smoking was making me even more anxious. It was stressful to go last, because I knew I would be comparing myself with all the other readers. Meanwhile, Eugene looked like the calmest person in the world, but when I asked if he was nervous, I saw how the cigarette trembled between his fingers. He was the first reader, and his poem was about an ex-girlfriend, and how he felt the first time he met her. As he was reading, he looked up at Elizabeth every once in a while. She actually didn't seem to be affected by it, but still, it was strange. I wish you'd been there, Effie, to help me figure out what was going on between those two.

After Eugene, a guy in a big, white gown read a poem while rolling oranges across the floor towards the audience. I was moved, even though I couldn't quite understand why. Through the window, I saw Elizabeth and Eugene talking. I remembered the way she looked at him that day at Rådhuspladsen when we met for the first time, and then I saw her rubbing his arm. An orange rolled over to my feet, and suddenly Elizabeth was back at my side, holding my hand. I watched Eugene, and when I made eye contact with him, I held it for a long time. I wanted him to see that she had come back to me.

When it was finally my turn, Elizabeth introduced me to the audience, and everyone looked in my direction expectantly. I tried to adjust the microphone so it wasn't too low. Then I took out my phone and opened the WhatsApp message with the poem that I'd sent to myself:

> I will steal a car
> drive out to the sea
> and though I never learned to swim
> I will find a boat
> sail
> out on the great sea
> here the fish god will meet me
> swim with me
> to a land where everything is burning
> then I will see
> that the water is safer
> and swim until I am home
> though I've never swum before
> I will wander through towns
> the sun will dry my clothes
> my body

my face
my hands
I will wander
past markets full of stalls
and libraries full of books
and schools full of children
in brown and yellow uniforms
recite the alphabet
walk past houses
where families eat their dinners
I will wander until I recognise everything
and I know that soon I'll be home
but home moves into me
and when I finally come home
I will wander out of town again
with new dreams and illusions
about once more feeling like a foreigner.

Fri 30 Sep

Hey Effie,

Does your baby sleep well at night? Are you getting your sleep? Are you happy?

Elizabeth insisted that I stay over at her place after the poetry reading yesterday. Sometimes I sleep on her sofa, even though I prefer to spend the night with the Crows. I was planning to go find them yesterday too, but there was something in Elizabeth's eyes that I hadn't seen before. I told her that I didn't need her to run a guesthouse just for me. Some of her friends were heading out to a bar, and I said she should go with them and have fun. She said it wasn't like she was asking me to move in or take care of her cat. It was refreshing to hear her tease me, like she does when we play basketball. I asked her a little nervously if she has a cat, because I can't stand those little beasts, and she said it was just a metaphorical cat. When we got to her building, she put her arm around mine and asked if I take my tea with milk and sugar. Yes to both, I said, and I told her how much I love tea with condensed milk. She lit up and said that was her biggest guilty pleasure. I asked her what a guilty pleasure was, which made her laugh.

My body ached when I saw her bed, as if all that comfort would be too hard to bear. When we walked into her living room, she said I could sit on the sofa while she made us tea. A spicy scent hung in the room, blending with Elizabeth's own smell of coconut oil. The walls were slanted and there were wooden beams in the ceiling, lots of books and green plants and posters and photographs taken in Africa. One of the photographs was of a man standing in a river with a big suitcase on his head, going somewhere. Elizabeth told me that her father took the picture in Senegal in the 1970s, and that it was that picture that made her want to be a photographer when she was little. Her apartment was full of proof that her childhood dreams had come true. There were rolls of film in the refrigerator, and in a cluttered little room full of clothes she had made space for a darkroom. Photographs from her job as a photojournalist were hung on a line to dry, held in place with clothespins. She showed me her photos proudly, and she said that when she's on assignment she sometimes takes analogue photos, even though she doesn't have to. She said she loves their tactile nature, and that she wants to capture moments that don't necessarily fit in with her assignments. She brought two cups to the table and set out milk, sugar and two spoons. It was the best tea that I've ever tasted, even without any condensed milk. She put some music on, Ethiopian jazz, she said, and leaned her head against my shoulder. She started asking me lots of questions, and she asked about you, too, Effie. She wanted to know what you look like, and what kind of clothes you wear. I told her that you always have stylish jeans on and braids in your hair, that you always wear pink, because it's your favourite colour.

When we woke up this morning, Elizabeth served us breakfast on her little balcony. It was full of herbs and potted plants, and I started thinking about the garden your new home will have, Effie. I felt guilty about wasting so much time with Elizabeth while the construction is still waiting to get started. I thought of hibiscus flowers and daisies, spider flowers and lilies, of ticking clocks and of my visa, which is slowly running out. But all the same, I had the wonderful sensation of actually being in the place I'd always dreamed of being, a place where I am wanted more than any other.

Sun 2 Oct

Effie!

This message might fall under the category of too much information, but bear with me.

I'm lying in Elizabeth's bed and we're a tangle of arms and legs. I don't know how to untangle myself. We were watching a film on her computer, but I couldn't concentrate, I couldn't stop staring at her. She noticed, and she said I should watch the film and not the pimples on her cheek. I took hold of her chin. I wanted to really see her, and I asked her not to look away. When I told her she was beautiful, she just giggled and looked at me sceptically. I caressed her face, took my time grazing her shoulders and arms and belly and hips with my hands, which must've felt like sandpaper against her soft skin. She slipped away from me, put on a kimono, and walked out of the bedroom. You're probably covering your eyes at this point, but I have to share this feeling with someone, I'm obsessed with her taste, her softness. She was so warm and nervous when I walked over to her in the doorway and took her hand. I slowly undressed her and pressed her up against the wall as I kissed her face, and without breaking our kiss, she started to back into the living room. I'd been trying in vain not to fantasise too much about being with her like this, but my imagination didn't even come close to reality. It was as if she wanted to be chased but never caught but she wouldn't dare admit it. We circled her coffee table for a long time, and when I caught up to her, she surrendered, and she asked me to kiss her again. When I lifted her chin and looked into her eyes, she looked away, and when I asked her to look at me, she seemed reluctant. But then she kissed me, and we were back together again, she practically clung to me, as if we were hanging off a cliff and I was the one who had to pull us up.

Effie, one time when we were younger and sitting under the blanket with Dad's torch, you asked me how to kiss, and I told you it was like eating a melting ice cream cone, you have to go about it carefully but urgently. Then you turned off the torch and ran away with your hands over your ears. But afterwards, you kept asking questions about all kinds of things, especially boys. What do boys think about girls? What makes girls attractive to them? You asked me these questions, and I have to confess, I didn't give you honest answers. What I didn't tell you is that we men have thoughts that we're ashamed of, thoughts about girls and women, thoughts about teachers and housemaids and other people's mothers and our friends' sisters. I'd thought so much about Elizabeth that I sometimes worried she could hear my thoughts, or smell how dirty they were. When I've been with her lately, I hardly dared to think at all out of fear that beasts would emerge from the rubbish bins of my mind and attack her, drag her down into the muck.

Wed 5 Oct

Hi Effie,

I've hardly left Elizabeth's bed for three days straight. She snores more than you. Do you remember how after our parents died, I was afraid to fall asleep at night, and it helped to listen to your snoring? In one of my recurring childhood dreams, we were both riding on a grasshopper into a soft night; I still think about that all these years later.

Femi just sent me a message asking if I could meet him and Kofi in the park and help film a dance routine that they've been working on. The other day he triumphantly confided in me that the girl they were both wild about was now writing to him, and only him. But he said it felt strange to keep it secret from Kofi. Maybe asking me to come help with their dance is his way of saying he misses me, but I don't think I want to leave Elizabeth today.

Sat 8 Oct

Dear Effie, Pastor, and Auntie,

I know it's been a long time since I wrote to all three of you, but something terrible has happened. I set off for Folkets Park today with a guilty conscience about the Crows, who I hadn't seen in weeks. As I got closer, I smelled smoke and saw blue lights and people crowding around under the trees. Fear struck me like lightning. There had been a fire and all the Crows' possessions lay charred and steaming, blackened to a crisp on the ground where we've slept and spent so many hours since we came to this country. Luckily, my things were all at Elizabeth's. Without thinking much about it, I've practically moved in with her since the poetry reading last month. But the other Crows lost all their clothes, everything went up in smoke along with their sleeping bags, sleeping mats, and photographs of their families. Luckily, they had their visas, passports and phones on them when it happened, and the twins also had their speakers. And no one got hurt, thank god.

An activist named Sonya came to the park to

help us. She's originally from Ghana, and she helps other African immigrants in the city by distributing sleeping bags and clothes that people have donated. Sonya is a small woman with a big presence, and she charged up to us asking all kinds of questions. She took detailed notes in her notebook while we told her about our situation, our visas from Italy, and the date that they expire.

Femi is nervous, because he thinks the fire was his fault. He got into a fight with a guy in the park yesterday. He doesn't want to tell us exactly what happened between them, but he says he blacked out with rage, and that he's ashamed.

Odofu wasn't with us in the park earlier, but when I texted him that someone had set our camp on fire, he just said we should forget about our possessions and get out of there as soon as possible. If the police found out about us, they would have to take us back to the station, and if that happened then we would be more vulnerable. They would have an excuse to keep an eye on us and periodically check our papers. I feel a simmering danger here in the city. You can't tell who's against you. The police are polite one moment and threatening the next. The gangs are just as unpredictable. They nod to us and mark their territory with index fingers shaped like pistols.

Sun 9 Oct

Dear Effie,

Sonya is an angel. She let Odofu and the twins move into her apartment temporarily after the fire. We're lying in their new room with smoke still clinging to our hair and our nerves. I couldn't bring myself to go back to Elizabeth's yesterday, it felt unfair, so I slept on a mattress beside Odofu.

Today I'm going out to collect bottles around schools in the city centre, but the fire has affected us all, and we're worried that we're on somebody's bad side. The twins are curled up together in the trundle bed beside Sonya's sons' old bunk bed. They're taking turns at online chess matches on their phone. A little while ago, Odofu broke the tension between us. He said he's been messaging with a woman in New Orleans. He sends her declarations of love, romantic songs, gifs with gleaming, blinking roses, and he ends all his messages with the words 'I miss you'. He's never met her, even though they've been writing to each other for two years now. The woman's name is Joan, she's sixty-seven years old, and she sends money to Odofu. He contacted her on Facebook, and now they write each other on Messenger. When I asked him if he feels guilty about it, he said that the dream of moving to the USA gives him energy, something to strive for. Joan's ex-husband left her for a younger woman and her children live in different states, far away from her. They're worried about her relationship with Odofu, especially since she sends him money, but he claims that it's actually the most honest kind of relationship imaginable, he and Joan and their messages built on the shared dream of a better life.

I started thinking about Elizabeth, and whether our relationship, or whatever it should be called, is comparable to Odofu's relationship with Joan. No matter what, Elizabeth will always be my life raft, and I will always be in her debt. She doesn't need me, even though she seeks me out. But I wish that she did need me, that there was something I could give her. I'm torn, because I love the fact that she wants to see me and wants to get to know me. But my whole life is made up of absences, and I don't want to bring her down with me.

Tue 11 Oct

Hi Effie,

I'm still crashing with the Crows at Sonya's apartment. Elizabeth and I meet in the city's public spaces, we kiss on the benches of Queen Louise's Bridge and the King's Garden, on the basketball courts and on swings in playgrounds. It feels like her way of being considerate to me. When we meet to play ball and kiss, we aren't confronted by our differences, other than the fact that she's a better basketball player than me. But I know she's making a deliberate effort to spare me from embarrassment. Except for bragging when she wins at basketball, she avoids reminding me of everything I don't have. In many ways, we are too considerate of each other, it narrows our options. She stands watch over my dignity, for better or worse.

Thu 13 Oct

Dear Pastor, Effie, and Aunt Dora,

Odofu started doing bike deliveries for a restaurant, and he just tipped me off that they might need somebody for cleaning and dishwashing.

When I got to Italy, I had all sorts of ideas about the kind of life a work visa would give me access to. The world was a place I had conquered, the sea was behind me, and the inertia I'd been living in for far too long had transformed into a liberating momentum. I dreamed of earning good money and experiencing a new country. In these dreams I built a house. I imagined that the work would give me the same sense of pride as the cashew plantation in Bono, an objective, a feeling of taking part in an important cycle. I didn't know that what awaited in the tomato fields of Italy was practically slave labour, but as soon as I signed the papers and received my work visa, I had this strange feeling, like I'd sold something but I wasn't sure what it was. A familiar anxiety set in when I saw that we would be freighted out to the fields by truck. This was the first warning sign, that we were being transported as if we were products. The truck had no windows and smelled of sweat, tomatoes, and hot skin. We sat in silence, packed in among stacks of green boxes with canned tomatoes in them. I had no idea how long we'd been sitting there. At one point, someone opened the door of the trailer, but the fresh air we hungered for was denied us. We heard voices outside, and I wondered if they could see us, but after the longest minute in the history of the world, the door closed again and the truck drove further out into the fields that are the blood vessels of Italy.

The sight of the farm was overwhelming. The tomato plants ran in rows that looked like endless lines of barbed wire with their gleaming red fruits, ready to be harvested and canned. Something in the air made me nervous, the faces, the grey knees, the bloodshot eyes, the workers moving like the living dead. I reminded myself that this was just a stepping stone, it was a job, a job in Italy. But we didn't have time to dwell on new surroundings. A Senegalese guy called us over and told us our job was to pick tomatoes from six in the morning until six at night without complaint. As he was giving us our instructions, Odofu shot me a sceptical look. We didn't know each other all that well at that point, but he was one of the men I crossed the sea with from Libya, and we had stuck together on the boat. I could tell Odofu was working up the courage to say something, and then he asked the Senegalese guy how much we were going to be paid for our work. I respected the fact that he was willing to risk his job on the very first day. We were told we would have to pay €5 for transportation to the fields, and for room and board, and after those expenses were covered we would earn € 2.50 for every full box of tomatoes.

An Italian-looking man with a bushy beard adorned the cans that the tomatoes were preserved in, and on the trucks that carried the tomatoes away from the fields there was a picture of someone who was supposed to look like he was doing our jobs. He stood in a fertile field in front of a truck with a wheelbarrow full of tomatoes and a warm smile on his face. But I didn't see any Italians during my time at the farm. They lived in a different world, and we had to cross the border that divided the tomato fields from their houses.

Regret lurched behind me like a long shadow as I moved through the flat landscape, picking tomato after tomato. The heat stung like a swarm of wasps, but no one dared to ask for a break, and we all just focused on our jobs from dawn to dusk. When the workday was over, we were freighted by bus to a place I never want to go back to. The camp consisted of low, primitive houses, and it reminded me of a village that had been razed to the ground in a civil war and abandoned. Most of the men there were from Central and West Africa, and up to twenty of us had to share the little rooms. We slept on dirty mattresses. There was no electricity, no running water. The men who enforced the merciless system of the farm were called capo nero, which means black boss in Italian. They took a cut of the money we paid every day for transportation and room and board, like a kind of tax. It was essentially impossible to earn enough money to survive and to send some home, too. Many of the men in the fields didn't have enough money to stay there, but they didn't have enough to leave either. No one revealed the truth about the job to their families.

Sat 15 Oct

Dear Pastor, Effie, and Aunt Dora,

I hope Pastor performed a naming ceremony for your baby, Effie. If only I could've been there. My thoughts keep returning to the day you were born, when Mum and Dad were still alive, and Auntie and Pastor came over for dinner every day. I remember how worried you were, Auntie, because the birth was taking so long and Mum was in so much pain, but when Effie came out she was so calm, as if Mum had given birth to peace itself. And I remember your naming ceremony, Effie, we had to wake up so early that day. It always takes place eight days after the birth. For the first seven days the mother needs to rest, but on the eighth day the whole house wakes up. The morning had just broken, the hens weren't clucking yet and Mum had a white shawl on her head as she walked through town with Effie in her arms. You, Auntie, walked at her side with Aunt Grace and the midwife, Augusta. Pastor, you were wearing your Kente cloth, and you welcomed the guests. Grandpa asked you to receive the gifts on

Augusta's behalf. She was given palm oil, a tray of yams, a bathing sponge, a handkerchief, and some money. Augusta thanked everyone for her gifts, and then Dad presented Mum with gifts: perfume, an evening dress, a pair of shoes, gold earrings, and the bracelet that Effie inherited later and never took off again. Pastor, you blessed the perfume, dabbed some of it on Mum's forehead and shoulders, and then you dabbed Effie in the same way. I remember wanting to be dabbed too, but I'd promised to be a good boy, so I kept quiet, watching on curiously as Grandma lifted Effie triumphantly into the air, as if she were a trophy. She did this three times as she recited the words: 'Have no fear, for you are protected.' And I will protect you, Effie. Every time I ask myself why I came to Europe, I remember this promise.

Sat 22 Oct

Dear Pastor, Auntie, and Effie,

I got the job! The one at the restaurant Odofu does bike deliveries for. Ironically, it's an Italian restaurant called Casa Mia. I've landed back in a little pocket of Southern Europe, but the wages are better than they ever were on the tomato farm, and they're also better than when I worked as a gardener and handyman for a family in Sicily who only paid me €1.50 per hour. My new job pays 68 kroner an hour, which is about €9. The work isn't all that demanding. I rinse off the dishes and put them into a big industrial dishwasher along with all the glasses and the silverware. When the restaurant closes, I've got the whole place to myself and I can listen to music. The walls are covered with old black-and-white photographs of men whistling at women, pictures of an Italy I never got to see. I have to bring my own supplies to the restaurant, but they didn't cost much, I just bought a mop, a bucket, rubber gloves, and some rags from Lidl; they have their own cleaning products. By the end of the month, I'll be able to pay for bricks, timber, and mortar for the house. Pastor, soon you'll be able to move my bed over to Effie's house, so you can set up the office you've always wanted for all your books and your daydreams.

Tue 25 Oct

Dear Effie,

Elizabeth had a big smile on her face as I walked towards her across the basketball court today. It was too cold and windy to play, but we met anyway, just to meet. Withered leaves covered the lines on the court. She threw her arms around my neck as if the wind had whirled her up to me. Her kiss was warm in the cold wind. There was no one else around. Only a few weeks ago, the park around the court was full of mothers with their babies, people walking on slacklines and practising acrobatic tricks, groups of friends drinking beer in the sun. Elizabeth's voice blew away with the wind, and she had to shout to tell me what was on her mind. She said she showed the photographs she took of me in Rådhuspladsen to her friend Haddy. I can't remember if I've told you about her, but she's one of Elizabeths oldest friends and she works in the fashion industry. And now Elizabeth says Haddy wants to cast me as a model in some fashion shows during Copenhagen Fashion Week. All I have to do is go to her agency and get some headshots taken. Elizabeth says she's sure that I would earn good money from the shows. It almost sounded too good to be true, but all the same, I agreed to meet Haddy the day after tomorrow in the hope of earning more money for your house. I have no idea what to wear. I wish you were here to help me. At least my clothes don't smell like rubbish anymore. Ever since I got the job at the restaurant, they've smelled like cleaning products.

Thu 27 Oct

Hi Effie,

I'm at the agency right now, looking at models. They're staring down at me from photographs on the walls. None of them are smiling, so I make a mental note not to smile when they call me into the office. People are going in and out in trendy outfits and they have good music on in the background, some French hip-hop. There are vases with flowers and green potted plants dotted around the room. Elizabeth loaned me her basketball jersey, which is too big for her but fits me just right, and I'm also wearing a pair of loose dress pants and Kofi's Air Jordans, which he normally refuses to take off, even in his sleep. Yesterday I went to see Lou, who had promised me a free trim, so now I look sharp. I showed up early so I wouldn't miss my appointment, making sure I wasn't operating on African time, as the twins call it whenever we make a plan to meet up.

I'm fascinated by the atmosphere around me, Effie. Just now, a guy came over and offered me sparkling water, which came straight from a faucet with a gushing sound. He asked if I liked my bubbles hard or soft, and now I'm drinking the water he gave me, but I still don't know exactly what it is that I asked for.

Tonight I have a shift at Casa Mia. All I can think about is that I don't want to lose that job. It feels like my only real hope for finishing your house right now, even though I'm sitting here trying to get this other job.

I just texted Elizabeth to tell her she owes me a dinner for this. She wrote back right away that she's the one doing me a favour. I reminded her that I haven't got the job yet, but then she wrote that what I'm doing now is just a formality, that I've already got it, I just need to get some neutral photos taken, which are easier to sell to customers because then they can imagine their own clothes when they look at me. And anyway, Haddy already booked me for a bunch of shows after she saw the photos from Rådhuspladsen.

Fri 28 Oct

Effie!

Listen to this. Yesterday when I stepped into Haddy's office at the fashion agency, five people were staring back at me. Haddy gave me a hug and said something in Danish to her colleagues, who nodded in agreement. She said everybody was so interested in my story. I asked what story she was talking about, and she said she meant my background as an asylum seeker. And even though I'm not actually seeking asylum here, I didn't say anything. I understood that this narrative was part of a strategy, and it was the reason I could look forward to earning the kind of money I'd never come close to earning before in my life. And all this for just putting on some clothes and walking down a runway! I answered politely that I was glad my story made a difference. Haddy looked at me expectantly. She had long nails with flames painted on them, and her T-shirt said 'Foreigners, please don't leave us alone with the Danes!' I couldn't focus on anything else. Then the guy from the lobby asked me if I wanted more sparkling water, which was grapefruit flavoured this time, and I finally tore my eyes away from Haddy's shirt. The guy took the opportunity to praise my face and my height, saying that I was athletic but I also had a poetic aura about me. They gave me a white T-shirt and a pair of black jeans to put on, and then they took lots of pictures of me, first with a big digital camera, then a Polaroid. I was sick with nerves. I wish Elizabeth had been there to help me stay calm. Then they asked me to walk back and forth like I would out on the runway, and a guy with blond hair and cowboy boots on demonstrated how I should move. They said I should be myself, but at the same time I had to keep my expression neutral so the focus would be on the clothes and not my face. It felt amazing to walk back and forth to the music in that big office, with sunlight crashing through the window like it was shining just for me. Haddy gave me instructions and asked me to move in certain ways, to walk and stand still, raise my chin a bit, walk again, spin around and walk. And then it was over, and I could go out into the fresh air.

It just occurred to me that I won't be able to put in any hours at Casa Mia during Fashion Week. I try to tell myself it doesn't matter, because now I'm going to earn enough money to really get the construction of your house going. As I was washing the floors late last night, I tried to remember all the things they taught me at the agency, but I'd already forgotten most of it.

Wed 2 Nov

Dear Effie,

Odofu watched me intensely as we drank our Cokes at a pizzeria. We were celebrating the twins' success on TikTok, where their dance videos are starting to get a lot of views, and also that Odofu and I have found jobs. But they only know about Casa Mia, I haven't mentioned the strange people who kissed me on the cheek and said 'hello darling' as if we were best friends. The Crows thought my happiness was all owing to the dishwashing job. I also moved back in with Elizabeth, but I haven't told them what it's like to sleep in her bed, or what it's like to be with her, how her body feels against mine. When Odofu asked about her, I tried to redirect our attention to him by asking him how he was doing. We haven't been close since autumn started sneaking up on us. Even though we have roofs over our heads and more regular jobs, we're still here on borrowed time, and with the cold comes a longing for everything back home.

Odofu revealed a big secret today. It turns out he's got a wife and two kids back home that he didn't tell us about. He has generally avoided telling us about the life he led before he travelled to Europe. Apparently, his wife confessed that she slept with another man, because she couldn't live without physical contact any longer. Now Odofu considers them as good as divorced. But his wife doesn't know what he went through during his journey to Europe or his time in Italy, because he wasn't honest about it. If she knew the details, maybe she would've seen his suffering as a testament to his love and stayed faithful to him. Now they're both miserable. She asked for his forgiveness, but he's hurt and angry and more determined than ever to unite with Joan in New Orleans, the very person who's been funding his wife's lifestyle and his children's tuition. Neither woman knows a thing about the other.

Fri 4 Nov

Dear Pastor,

A fashion show is like theatre. The models put on costumes and perform onstage. The audience consists of important people in their most beautiful clothes, seated in rows that delineate a hierarchy. They take videos of us with their phones, watching us only through screens and filters, and then share us with thousands of other people who were not invited. The fact that I'm among the invited is still hard to grasp. As a model, you have to do the exact opposite of what an actor does, you have to express as little as you possibly can. Pastor, when you drape yourself in your Kente cloth, when you walk among other men in parades adorned with gold, that is our version of a runway. Funerals, naming ceremonies and weddings are our versions of Fashion Week because these parties last for days and everyone in town puts their nicest clothes on. The difference is that everyone's invited.

The clothes I wear when I walk up and down the runway are new and without history. You've had the same Kente cloth as long as I can remember. You got it from your grandfather, my great-grandfather, who in turn got it from his father. But the fabric always looks new, no matter how many years pass. Every time I put on a new outfit at one of these shows, I feel like a different character. But when I take the clothes off, the character disappears. When you put on your costume, Pastor, with your rings, your bracelet, and your cloth, you become even more the person you already are.

Sat 5 Nov

Hey Effie,

I'm at a party and I wish you were here. I snuck into a toilet cubicle to write to you. Elizabeth has been trying to get hold of me all night, but I haven't answered. We had planned to meet up when I was done with the evening's shows. I rode part of the way on the back of a bike belonging to a girl I'd never even met. Then we hopped into the back of a taxi. There were disco lights and loud music in the car. When I left the apartment earlier, Elizabeth seemed sad. She's been saying all week that she felt insecure about all the models I'd meet and the attention I'd get. Maybe she's afraid I'll pull away from her. She says she's happy for me that I'm getting the money and the experience, but she can't hide the fact that something's wrong. A few hours ago, she texted me that she was standing outside the entrance of the party, but the doorman wouldn't let her in because she wasn't on the guest list. I don't know why, but I pretended not to see her message and put my phone back in my pocket.

Sun 6 Nov

Dear Pastor, Auntie, and Effie,

The birds are flocking south, and the very same leaves that shaded us from the sun a few months ago as we slept in the parks are letting go of the trees and whirling away. Now the trees are sleeping. Autumn has retreated and given way to winter. The people in the city are wrapped up in long coats and down jackets, not nearly as sociable in the cold winds as they were during the red and orange fashion show of late summer and autumn. It's like the city is steadily closing in on itself.

Mon 7 Nov

Dear Effie,

Elizabeth's bed is smeared in my gold makeup from yesterday. I'm lying beside her, playing with the pendant on her necklace. She seems withdrawn since I blew her off the other night. I'm going to model at more shows over the next few days and earn so much money it makes me dizzy. 5,000 kroner for a single show. I haven't been earning enough since Elizabeth and I got together, so this is like a gift from the heavens. I haven't had the courage to tell her that the construction of your house would come to a standstill if this modelling job hadn't come to my rescue.

I want to wake Elizabeth up and tell her about the jobs I had to take before I came to Copenhagen, to open up about the life I ran away from with the Crows. But I'll settle for telling you, Effie. I just don't want to ruin things between me and her. Last night I carried her from the sofa over to the bed after she fell asleep. It can't always be her carrying me.

Thu 10 Nov

Dear Effie and Dora,

I need your advice. Elizabeth is acting cold, and I'm trying to get back into the warmth. I invited her to play basketball today, hoping for redemption. She dribbled proudly and beat me without batting an eyelid. I looked like a complete amateur. Leaves still covered the lines on the asphalt and lots of chestnuts had fallen, scattered around like little traps. At one point I slipped on one and fell flat on my butt. Elizabeth thought it was hilarious, but I got right back up, pretended I was walking a runway leading straight to her, and kissed her. I held her close even though it felt a little awkward.

I know I haven't treated her well lately. I just need a better understanding of women. I can't allow myself to offer nothing while she gives me everything. I want to be worthy of her love. Effie and Auntie, tell me everything there is to know about being a woman! Tell me about all your unrequited crushes!

Sat 19 Nov

Dear Pastor, Effie, and Dora,

The twins have been sending me silly videos about the strict childrearing by West African parents compared to laidback Europeans. In one of them, a mother cross-examines her daughter because she's lying in bed relaxing. She gives her daughter a lecture about everything she ought to be doing instead of lounging around. Beds weren't soft when I was young, the mother says, they were made of fire, so we knew how to get off our asses. We laugh on opposite ends of the city. Outside Elizabeth's window the rain is endless.

Next week she's travelling to Athens on assignment. It's her first one from a big Danish newspaper, but she keeps asking if she should just drop it and stay with me. It's like she's afraid I'll disappear if she looks away. She's working on a photo-series about athletes who don't win. Photographers tend to focus on the winners, strong legs overtaking the competition, running to victory in a storm of flashing lights. That's where the money is. But Elizabeth wants to capture the feelings of the athletes who lost the gold by a hair's breadth. The look in their eyes the moment they cross the finish line and realise they didn't come in first. She already photographed a number of black, female 100-metre runners from Jamaica and the US when she was at the Olympics in the States, and now she's going to Greece, birthplace of the Olympic games. Greece is also one of the countries that receives the most migrants, and Elizabeth believes that their journey across the Mediterranean Sea is in itself an athletic feat worthy of documenting. I can feel a growing distance between what she photographs and my own experience of what she photographs.

I don't like being in the apartment without her, so I'm going to stay at Sonya's while she's gone. I've made my decision, but she thinks it's silly and she seems hurt. 'I like knowing you're in my home, that it could also be yours,' she told me when I refused her offer. But I just said I'd promised the twins and Odofu to help out with their meal deliveries. That's not entirely true, but it's not entirely false either. I can tell that they still want me to spend more time with the group, so I'm going to try to see them a bit more while Elizabeth is away. She said she understood, but I'm not sure she does. We're all so anxious at the moment. It's only a matter of time until our visas run out, and then we'll really have to start looking over our shoulders.

Tue 22 Nov

Dear Effie,

I'm writing to you from the mattress in Sonya's apartment, right beside a snoring Odofu. The twins have started taking night shifts at their cleaning job and they hardly get any sleep. They make meal deliveries from morning to evening and most nights they clean as well. They want to go to Paris, but that will take a lot of money. They haven't been making nearly as many videos lately, they're dancing less. Elizabeth has been sending me long, detailed messages from Athens. Her main focus there is the migrants coming in by boat along the coast. She wrote that she misses me and looks forward to seeing me again, and that the African Christmas party is coming up.

By the way, I haven't been hired for any more modelling jobs. Fashion Week was literally a one-week dream. Haddy hasn't answered my texts asking if there's any more work for me.

I've been thinking a lot about your child, Effie. Can it already crawl around on the beach and look for turtles in the sand, or is it still just a little

bundle on your back as you walk in the garden,
Aunt Dora by your side?

Mon 28 Nov

Dear Effie,

Elizabeth is home again. She hadn't even put her bags down before she started telling me everything about her trip. She alternated between kissing me and talking so fast she tripped over her words.

One night, she got a ride out to Malakasa to document the migrants landing on the beach in orange rubber boats just like the one I took on my journey to Italy. When she showed me her photographs, I could taste the salt water and my forehead got hot. The photographs are beautiful, Effie, but there's nothing beautiful about those people's fate. The beauty is practically an insult, but Elizabeth is proud of her work. She told me the names of the people she photographed, and it was clearly a moving experience for her. But a photograph reveals and obscures at the same time. When I walked the runway with lights flashing in my eyes, I wasn't thinking about the pictures of me that are now floating around out there somewhere, pictures that have nothing to do with who I am. They were always telling me how good-looking and unique I was, but what did that actually mean?

Elizabeth showed me a picture of a mother holding her child, wrapped in a golden blanket. It shone like a beautiful cape, and the mother's ebony skin gleamed in the sun. Elizabeth looked at me with a hopeful expression, eager to hear what I thought of her photos, and all I could say was that they were beautiful.

As Elizabeth told me about her trip, I had an unwelcome feeling of envy. Her insights into these people's lives were acquired at a distance. She is free to travel out into the world and then return home. But I kept it to myself, told her I was proud of her. Then I gave her a long kiss. She's put on a little weight, and I think it suits her.

Thu 1 Dec

Dear Effie,

I often think back to the day Mum and Dad drove off. It was the most beautiful day. We had spent it making food for Uncle Kwame's funeral and decorating for the party. Our dad was going to bury his youngest brother. He was wearing Kwame's cap, the one with the Coca-Cola logo that he always had on. Its brim was smudged with oil. Kwame was a mechanic before he got sick. My fingers were sticky with pineapple juice. You were wearing Dora's dress, the one she sewed herself. My suit was too big, and I'd insisted that Yao cut my hair like a rapper from LA. Mum and Dad wanted to grill fish, and our neighbour Charles knew a fisherman with good prices.

Before they drove away, Mum squeezed me tight. Sometimes I lean into that last embrace, her warm cheek and her short, soft hair grazing my shoulder. The scent of her stayed with me for years. That moment often comes back to me like a mosquito bite, a throb in my chest. I prolong those hours in my thoughts, preparing the fish and chopping the pineapples. I lean into that day like it will never end. That day is the one that holds all the others up. The day Mum and Dad died smelled of pineapples. It smelled of death.

I can't really remember our childhood anymore. I can't remember whether the TV was by the window in the living room or closer to the kitchen. I can't remember whether our bathtub was blue or green. Dad's scar, I can't remember whether it was on his left or right cheek. I can't remember our teacher Tina's eyes, but I do remember her orange dress, and the way it hugged her breasts. I can't remember the seats in our car. Were they made of vinyl or leather?

Sat 3 Dec

Dear Effie,

I haven't spent the night at Elizabeth's since she came home. We both go about our lives in this little city, but our paths never seem to cross. Maybe it's on purpose. But I was relieved when she wrote to me that the Christmas party was right around the corner and I should take out my dancing shoes. She asked if I would DJ for a while at the party, and if Femi and Kofi might want to do a dance performance.

Mon 5 Dec

Dear Effie,

December brought in the snow. A white blanket lies heavy over all the cars and rooftops, the pavements and trees. It's funny that snow is cold, because it looks so warm and soft. When I brush the white powder off of my bike seat in the morning, I wonder if it might be time to move on. Maybe the party's over. The northerners have all barricaded themselves indoors from now until the return of spring. But today, for just a moment, I forgot all about how life is a serious thing, how there's no longer any money to be earned here, how we're under pressure and afraid of being deported. Elizabeth and I made snow angels in Ørstedsparken wearing snowsuits she got at a charity shop. We looked like idiots.

Wed 7 Dec

Dear Effie,

Odofu won't stop talking about what clothes we should wear to the Christmas party tomorrow. I want to look sharp. Maybe I'll buy a chequered shirt and a pair of Levi's. But I should probably save the money for Christmas presents for you all. Odofu is very vain, and his vanity extends to us as well. He knows that the Danes like dressing in black. 'It's easier to look clean in black,' he says whenever I beg for permission to wear colours and patterns that lift the mood. Now he wants a Hugo Boss shirt and a pair of stylish, pointy shoes.

I hope Elizabeth likes my shirt. I think about her all the time, but I force myself not to text her at night, when I'm at my loneliest. Why should she be with someone like me, someone with nothing to offer? I can't take her out to restaurants or travel the world with her. We can't put down roots. I can't provide for her. I can't even split the expenses. All she can have is me and my soul, my empty pockets and my restlessness.

Fri 9 Dec

Hi Effie,

The party yesterday was a light in the dark of winter. The People's House was full to the brim, and there was a chaotic buzz in the main hall. There were kids and adults and lots of the men I've seen biking around the city with bottles. I also saw people I recognised from the protest in Rådhuspladsen and the poetry reading. I could hear Sonya's voice the whole time. She reminds me of Aunt Dora in a lot of ways. Sturdy and warm, a powerful little storm. Elizabeth was bringing out the last trays of food. I watched her for a long time before she finally noticed me and waved. When the food was ready, she sat beside me at a long table, and it was a relief to be close to her. But the smells of the Jollof rice and the different meat stews and big piles of fufu distracted me. I ate like I was in a trance. Big platters swelled with food on the long tables. Rice, banku, and fried fish, peanut sauce with chicken, injera pancakes, and different kinds of dip, spinach, lentils, and chili in big bowls with little, round Ghanaian bofrot doughnuts. My belly cried out for it all, and I tried to control my hunger and eat less ravenously, but you know me, when I'm eating I basically black out. My mouth was full of chicken when Elizabeth scooted her chair closer to mine. She tried to break through my food coma by asking about my plans for the new year. I'm so tired of lying and dodging, Effie. I said that I honestly had no idea, that I've been trying to avoid thinking about it. I tried to seek refuge in her face, and I told her she looked beautiful. She seemed hurt. I tried to suppress my desire to touch her neck and the fabric of her dress, and instead I asked her if she wanted to dance.

Some female DJs were playing too much Fela Kuti, so Sonya made them relinquish control of the booth and took over herself. Turns out, she's an excellent DJ, which made me even more nervous about the fact that it was my turn soon. I was so scared that the dance floor would come to a standstill. Just like when I was waiting to read at the poetry night, I wanted to get it over with.

An hour later, a DJ app was spinning on the screen of my phone. Femi and Kofi had helped me download Turntable, so I could crossfade between the songs on my playlist. I was nervous, but I started with Yemi Alade's 'Johnny'. Everyone sang along, and I kept looking for Elizabeth out on the dancefloor, especially when I played 'Playboy' by Fireboy DML and 'Only Man She Want' by Popcaan. I left the DJ booth while the song was playing, got down on my knees in front of her, and then got up and gave her the kiss of a lifetime.

Wed 14 Dec

Dear Effie, Auntie, and Pastor,

The snow has transformed from a soft blanket over the city to sooty, slushy mud that clings to my shoes and makes them filthy. The money for your house, Effie, the money I earned at the fashion shows, is wrapped up in wads and hidden in a secret place. That money is carpenters, concrete, and shingles. It is bricks and mortar. I will build you a paradise.

Pastor Emanuel, you once told me the colonial powers led our forefathers to believe that the heavens were overcrowded, that there wasn't room for our people in their elegant quarters. So we were homeless and restless and we searched every nook and cranny for a place of our own, only to discover that there were chambers under the ground. You told me our forefathers live down there, and when we cry, we nourish the earth in the subterranean gardens of paradise. When we die, our blood turns to fertile soil.

In my head, Paradise is a place of singing trees. But in many African religions, there's no distinction between the spiritual and the earthly. The spirit world exists alongside us. It moves into us, stays with us throughout our lives, and adds new dimensions and layers to our existence. You said: The dead are living, Cosmos. There is no place to long for in the hereafter. Heaven is right here. When we die, we wander on invisibly as if nothing had happened at all.

Sat 17 Dec

Dear Effie,

Before you were born, Dad took me with him one day to Cape Coast. Every once in a while, we would go on trips together, mostly to Lomé Grand Market where we bought things for Aunt Dora's stall: buckets, shower heads, chewing gum, chocolate, all sorts. But one day, we made the long drive to Cape Coast and the city of his childhood, Elmina. He wanted to show me around, to show me why he became a fisherman. He wanted to pass on his dream of a good life.

They still take great pride in their fishing industry in Elmina, and the big fish market is the city's epicentre. The women play a central role there, they send their men, their sons, and their fathers out to sea, knowing full well that they might not come back again. When the fishermen come home with their boats full of One Man Thousand, they work with the women in a kind of guild, drying and selling the fish together. They are the queens of the market. Together, they cook the food over outdoor fireplaces, then they carry big tubs of fish on their heads to stalls at the harbour front and the surrounding villages to sell them. The way the women work creates a special atmosphere in the big marketplace, a sense of community and a hum of activity I haven't felt before or since. It was the women of Elmina market who taught Dad to mend fishing nets and to dry fish. The men may bring the fish home, but it is the women who transform them into meals, into life, into gathering.

Dad told me that he rarely saw his own father when he was a child, but he could always count on the women of the family; they were ever-present. Men go charging out into the world, out to sea, with the notion that they are important. In Elmina, my father tried to show me that somebody has to stay back on land, and that men forget to see the life they go charging away from as valuable. Maybe I should've learned something from our trip to the fish market that day.

A plane is leaving its trail across the sky as I write this message to you, which I know you'll never read. I wonder what it's like to fly. Elizabeth is calling me. In another life, she and I will be two crows flying high above the world, high above everything that no one owns.

Sat 24 Dec

Dear Effie,

My name is Elizabeth Adu. I wish you a merry Christmas, and I'm writing on behalf of your brother, Cosmos. He's told me so much about you that it feels like I'm sitting right next to you as I write this message. Outside the window, snow is lying on the rooftops like icing on gingerbread houses. My whole family is gathered in the kitchen, arguing about the food, the smell of roast duck has filled the house, and I'm seeking refuge in my childhood bedroom.

My hands are shaking a little, because it's hard to explain who I am to Cosmos. I never quite managed to figure that out during the time that I knew him. I suppose we were like boyfriend and girlfriend. I met Cosmos this past summer, in Copenhagen, after his difficult time in Italy. He had travelled here with three friends to work and earn money to build you a house. He would type on his phone every day, deep in thought, but he would never tell me who he was writing to. Only now do I understand why he lay awake so often at night, typing away, his phone lit up in the darkness beside me. Only now, after reading those messages, do I understand how important it was for him to write to you and be connected with you. But I also understand that it was too hard for him to actually send them.

Cosmos left behind his phone, the money for your house, and meticulous instructions about how to deposit the money in the bank and then send it to you using Revolut, which you'll need to download. I'm forwarding you the messages he wrote to you but sent only to himself, so that you will know where he's been, and how he was. I love him, but I could never bring myself to say it to him, for fear that I'd have to acknowledge that I couldn't keep him. I want to pass on the love I could never really show him to you all, to his family, and to his home.

He never told me what it cost him to be away from you all, but he talked about you all the time, Effie. I think I reminded him a little of you. I tried to imagine your face as I read about you, your aunt Dora, and your uncle, Pastor Emanuel. If you look like your brother, you have dark brown eyes and a face like a landscape with rivers one yearns to swim in and soft soil one yearns to touch. If you look like your brother, there are secrets in your eyes; if you look like your brother, you are a temple of wonders; if you look like your brother, you are beautiful.

As I write to you, I have one hand on my belly. A new life is growing inside of me, and my happiness is mixed with my anxiety at not knowing where Cosmos is, if he's all right, or if I'll ever see him again. Part of me hopes he's on his way home to you and your aunt and uncle. If he comes back to you, I'm sure he'll show you that he's not afraid to swim anymore, that he loves your child and would do anything to take care of you both. If he comes home to Woe, will you promise to tell him that he will become a father next summer? I'm sending a photograph from the day I met him. It was an important day. The laces of one of his shoes had come undone. The photo was taken the moment before he looked at me in a way no one has ever looked at me before. It was taken when we were still strangers.

A midwife scanned my belly a few days ago, so I'm also sending a photo of the little picture of the foetus, so you'll know that it's real, that we are, in a way, related now. I think it looks like a little bean, a bean that will one day become a baby that will grow up. I can hardly imagine it. Part of me is scared that it won't ever become a child, that it will just grow inside me like an empty space after Cosmos, and that the child, just like him, will disappear. I know I want to keep it.

Effie, I hope you are well. I hope one day I'll get to come and see your house, and our children will run down to the sea to catch turtles, like Cosmos told me the two of you did in your childhood.

Many loving thoughts,
Elizabeth

We ensure all our products comply with GPSR, CE marking, and other applicable EU Directives. Our EU Responsible Person for GPSR product safety compliance is EU Compliance Partner.

EU Responsible Person (EU RP):
EU Compliance Partner

Postal address: Pärnu mnt. 139b – 14, 11317 Tallinn, Estonia

Contact Email: hello@eucompliancepartner.com

Website: www.eucompliancepartner.com

Phone: +33757690241